Can I Pray with My Eyes Open?

Susan Taylor Brown & *Illustrated by* Garin Baker

HYPERION BOOKS FOR CHILDREN & *New York*

Printed in Hong Kong.

FIRST EDITION

5 7 9 10 8 6

This book is set in 24/30-point Calisto.
The art for this book was executed in oil paint.

℘

Library of Congress Cataloging-in-Publication Data

Brown, Susan (Susan Taylor).
Can I pray with my eyes open?/Susan Brown; illustrated by Gavin Baker—1st. ed.
p. cm.
Summary: In rhyming text, a child wonders how and when and where is the perfect way
to say a prayer and realizes that there is no wrong time or place for prayer.
ISBN 0-7868-0328-2 (trade)—ISBN 0-7868-2273-2 (lib. ed.)
1. Prayer—Juvenile literature. [1. Prayer.] I. Baker, Gavin, ill. II. Title.
BL560.B66 1999
291.4'3-dc21   98-51676

For my mother, Darlene Tennell,

who never stops giving me second chances. Thanks, mom.

—S. T. B.

❦

The work done in this book is dedicated to my family—

Jerilyn, Amanda, and Harrison—who patiently posed and inspired me.

Can I Pray With My Eyes Open? gave me an opportunity to preserve,

with paintings, a fleeting moment in our children's young lives,

when excitement, joy, and questions go hand in hand.

—G. B.

I wondered how and when and where
was the perfect way to say a prayer.

Must every prayer
be one that's spoken?
And can I pray
with my eyes open?

When I go swimming in the creek,
or play a game of hide-and-seek,

Or even when I climb a tree,
if I'm outside, can You hear me?

When I'm under the covers, out of sight,
or listening to music or flying a kite,

When I don't know
what I should do,
is that a time
to talk to You?

If I cross my fingers or stand on my head,
or get mad and my face turns red,

When I Rollerblade or ride my bike,
can I pray any time I like?

If I'm skipping rope or playing ball,
or walking backward down the hall,

When building castles at the beach,
will You still be within my reach?

When I look up and count the stars,
or climb upon the monkey bars,

When I'm in a car, a boat, or train,
does every prayer have to be the same?

I thought it over
through and through.
Then I shared
my thoughts with You.

I got an answer right away. . . .
There's no wrong time or place to pray.